For my friends and Avant-Guardian Angels.
With special thanks to Leslie Harris. — N. L.

Book design by Jennifer West.
Typeset in Bernhard Gothic, Keedy Sans and Retrofit.
The illustrations in this book were rendered in gouache.
Manufactured in Hong Kong.

Library of Congress Cataloging-in-Publication Data
Laden, Nina.
When Pigasso met Mootisse / by Nina Laden.
p.   cm.
Summary: Pigasso, a talented pig, and Mootisse, an artistic bull, live across the road from one
another, but when conflicts arise they build a fence that ultimately becomes a modern art
masterpiece. Includes biographies of the real-life artists, Henri Matisse and Pablo Picasso.
ISBN-10: 0-8118-1121-2   ISBN-13: 978-0-8118-1121-7
1. Matisse, Henri, 1869-1954. [1. Pigs—Fiction. 2. Bulls—Fiction.
3. Artists—Fiction. 4. Picasso, Pablo, 1881-1973. 5. Humorous stories.] I. Title.
PZ7.L13735Wh   1998
[E]—dc21   98-2611   CIP

20 19 18 17 16 15

Chronicle Books LLC
680 Second Street, San Francisco, California 94107

www.chroniclekids.com

When Pigasso met Mootisse

by Nina Laden

chronicle books · san francisco

There once was a young pig named **Pigasso**. While the other piglets
rolled in the mud and played games, Pigasso painted.
He painted anything and everything, and in
a most unusual way.

At the same time, there once was a young bull named **Mootisse**. Mootisse was not like the other bulls. He wasn't interested in bull fighting. Mootisse was happy only when he painted pictures. And he painted

big. bold. bright pictures.

In time, word of Pigasso's talent spread throughout the pig provinces. Soon, **art loving pigs** from all over lined up to buy his creations.

At the same time, Mootisse was getting famous in the cattle community. There weren't many households that didn't own a "**Moosterpiece**."

Pigasso and Mootisse were becoming art superstars.
But this came with a price. Everybody wanted to see them:
art buyers, art sellers, art students, art historians, art groupies.

It was an art attack!

One day Pigasso got fed up and said, "I'm tired of this **noisy pig pen**."

At the same time Mootisse declared, "I'm sick of this **crowded cow town**."

Needing a change, they both decided to look for a peaceful place where they could paint without distractions.

So each of the two artists looked far and wide for the perfect spot. Pigasso found a lovely farm looking towards the east. Mootisse found a handsome farm facing the west. After Pigasso moved in, he went to introduce himself to his new neighbor across the road.

At the same time, Mootisse went to introduce himself to his new neighbor across the road. That is how Pigasso met Mootisse.

And coincidentally,

that is how Mootisse met Pigasso.

At first, Pigasso and Mootisse were friendly
and welcomed each other as neighbors.
But soon, things began to change.

It started one day when Pigasso criticized one of Mootisse's paintings. Then Mootisse made fun of one of Pigasso's.

Mootisse called Pigasso an "**Art Hog**." Then Pigasso called Mootisse a "**Mad Cow**."

Mootisse quipped, "You paint like a **two year old**." Pigasso retorted, "You paint like a **wild beast**."

Mootisse raged, "Your colors look like **mud**." Pigasso spat, "Your paintings look like **color-by-numbers**!"

Then things got really out of hand.

It was a
modern art mess.

Pigasso stormed off into his house. "That Mootisse doesn't like my art," he **huffed**. "Well, I'll show him."

And Mootisse bullied his way into his house. "I'll give that Pigasso something he can really criticize," he **snorted**.

Then a full-scale feud erupted. But it was a most unusual battle. Armed with ladders and buckets of paint, Mootisse launched the first attack. He started at dawn. By the end of the evening he had succeeded in transforming the outside of his house into a monster-sized "**Moosterpiece**."

Not to be outdone, Pigasso fired up his paint brushes and, in full view of the enemy, counter-attacked. He turned his farm into a huge and outrageous "**Pork of Art**."

The two artists then retreated into their houses and pulled down the shades. Pigasso certainly didn't want to look out his window and stare at a "**Mootisse**." And Mootisse had no desire to give his rooms a view of a "**Pigasso**."

This presented a problem.
And there seemed to be
only one solution.

Without a word to each
other, Pigasso and Mootisse
each began to build a
huge wooden fence down
the middle of their road.

At first, Pigasso and Mootisse seemed satisfied. Both artists went back to painting by themselves. But after awhile, Pigasso was surprised to find that he missed that bull-headed Mootisse. At the same time, Mootisse found his studio empty without the presence of pig-headed Pigasso.

Pigasso pondered, "That Mootisse isn't such a bad artist. He has some interesting ideas."

Mootisse moaned, "That Pigasso
may not paint like me, but he
knows what he's doing."

However, being naturally **pig-headed** and **bull-headed**, neither artist knew how to apologize to the other. So they did what they do best. They let their paint brushes do the talking.

Pigasso painted on one side of the fence, and Mootisse painted on the other. Each worked until they were exhausted. It was strangely quiet when they were done.

Then, curious to see what Mootisse had been doing, Pigasso sprinted around to the other side. At the same time, Mootisse galloped over to Pigasso's side.

The silence was broken
as the two artists began laughing
at their amazing
work of heart.

From that day on, Pigasso and Mootisse became great friends.
They happily took down the fence and shared their different views.
A few months later, a big museum bought the fence.

Pigasso called his side: "**When Pigasso Met Mootisse**."

Mootisse called his side: "**When Mootisse Met Pigasso**."

The critics called it "Incredible."

The True Story of Picasso and Matisse

Picasso and Matisse were not a pig and a bull. But they **were** characters! They were two of the finest artists of the twentieth century. While they were never neighbors, they became close in the small world of art.

Henri Matisse was born on December 31, 1869, in France. Matisse didn't want to be an artist when he was little. He studied to be a lawyer. But when he was twenty-one, he got sick with appendicitis. While he was getting better, he painted his first painting. He liked painting so much that he ended his law career.

Pablo Picasso was born on October 25, 1881, in Spain. His father was an art teacher who helped Picasso start painting when he was very young. It was soon obvious that he was very talented. Picasso studied painting in Barcelona and Madrid, two big cities in Spain. But as he was growing as an artist, Picasso decided to move to Paris, which was, and still is, a great city for art. That is where Picasso met Matisse.

Picasso

Matisse

Both Picasso and Matisse were gaining recognition as artists in Paris. In fact, two Americans named Leo and Gertrude Stein, who lived there, started collecting their paintings. In 1906, Gertrude Stein had a party, and that is where Picasso and Matisse met for the first time.

At first, Picasso and Matisse were friendly to each other. They even traded paintings. Matisse also gave Picasso an African mask which inspired him to paint in a primitive style, a style he became very famous for. But soon it became apparent that Picasso and Matisse were becoming rivals and competitors. Picasso said some bad things about Matisse's paintings... and Matisse said some bad things about Picasso's. But, over time, the two artists learned to respect each other and became life-long friends. They both owned many of each other's paintings.

Matisse once told Picasso, "We must talk to each other as much as we can. When one of us dies, there will be some things the other will never be able to talk of with anyone else."

Matisse died in 1954. Picasso died in 1973. But their art lives on in many museums, galleries, and private collections around the world.

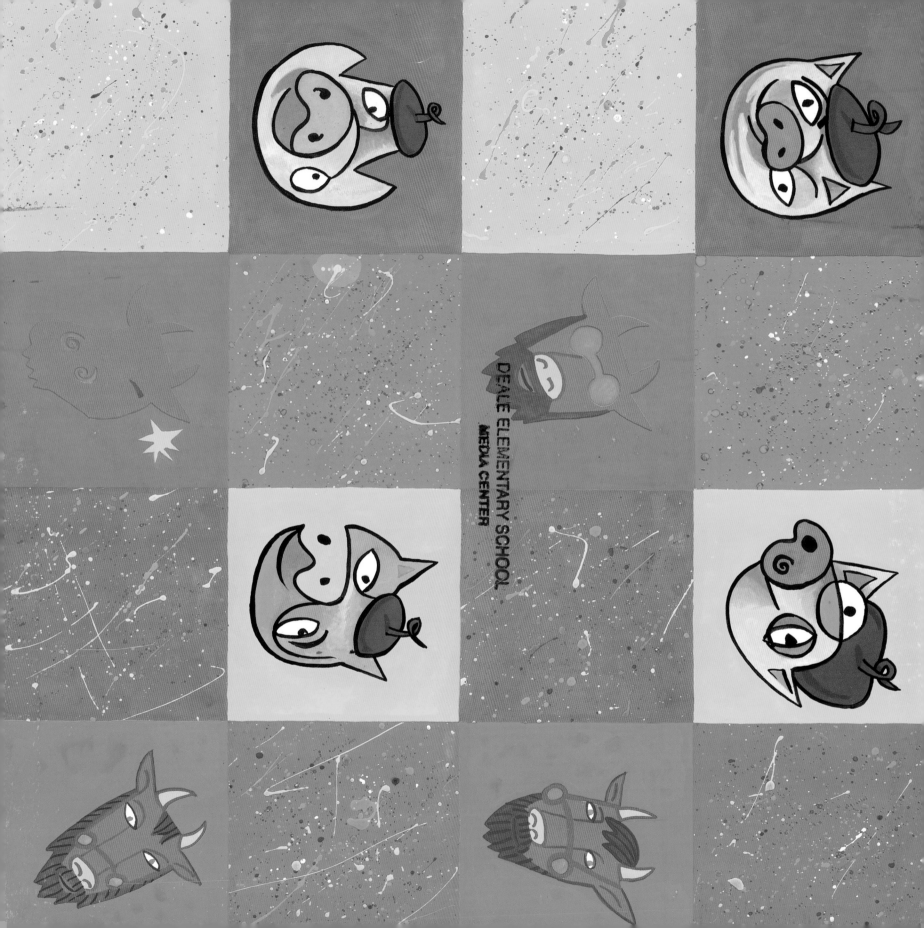

DEALE ELEMENTARY SCHOOL
MEDIA CENTER